Postman Pat® and the
Pink Slippers

It had been raining in Greendale and there were puddles everywhere.

"Whoa! Mind that puddle, Jess," said Pat, as he loaded up his post van.

"Oh, wait a minute, Pat," called Mrs Goggins, "you've forgotten this parcel. It's for Ted Glen."

"Oh, thank you, Mrs Goggins. What a strange shape! I wonder what it is?"

At school the children were learning all about fruit and vegetables.

"You should try and eat at least five pieces of fruit or vegetables every day to be healthy," said Mr Pringle.

"I love fruit," said Meera.

"Well, that's great, because we're going on a fruit hunt."

"I don't really like fruit, sir," said Julian.

"Oh, I'm sure you'll find something you like," replied Mr Pringle.

When Pat arrives at Ted Glen's he has to dodge the big puddles.

"Is that you, Pat?" calls Ted. He opens the door suddenly, Pat steps back, right in to a big puddle, splashing Jess.

"You've got the parcel. It's the final part for my new invention."

Pat looks down at his feet. "Oh, no... now my feet are soaking wet!"

"Wet feet?" chuckled Ted. "I've got just the thing for that. Take those wet shoes and socks off and I'll be back in a minute."

"I can't be too long, Ted," replied Pat. "I've only just started my rounds."

Pat sits down wringing the water out of his socks. "Ugh! Wet socks!"

"Miaow!" Jess replied.

Meanwhile, the children were picking blackberries with the Reverend Timms.

"Blackberries are my favourite fruit," said Tom.

"And mine!" Katie said.

"I don't really like blackberries, Mr Pringle," said Julian.

"Don't worry, Julian. We're going to Thompson Ground now. There's bound to be some fruit there that you like."

At the watermill, Ted wheels in his new invention.

"Ta-dah! It's a sock dryer! Your socks will be completely dry in seconds... just put them in here and away we go!"

"Er... is it supposed to smoke like that, Ted?" asked Pat.

"Eh? Oh, no! I'm sorry, Pat."

"Now I've got holey socks and wet shoes! I can't finish my rounds like this," said Pat.

"Don't worry," replied Ted. "I'm sure I can find some spare shoes you can wear."

At Thompson Ground Bill brings over two enormous melons.

"Look at these! Dad said we could have them from the greenhouse. You wait until you try them, Julian."

"I don't really like melon. It's too watery," Julian said.

"But this is the best melon you've ever tasted…"

Meanwhile, Ted had found some dry shoes.

"Pink slippers?" enquired Pat.

"Er... sorry Pat, I've looked everywhere but I've nowt else," replied Ted.

Pat sighed. "Oh, well, I'm sure they'll be fine. How do I look?"

"Grand!" Ted chuckled.

"Miaow!"

When Dr Gilbertson arrived at the orchard the children were busy picking fruit.

"Hello, what are you all up to?"

"Hello, mum," said Sarah. "We're on a fruit hunt."

"We've got to pick as many different types of fruit as we can," Julian said.

"Mr Thompson said we could pick his plums, and the apples," said Lucy.

"Oh, what an excellent idea," said Dr Gilbertson. "Fruit is very good for you."

"It's isn't much fun for me," Julian sighed, "I don't like any fruit."

"Don't you like apples or plums, Julian?" Dr Gilbertson asked.

"Not really."

Suddenly lots of apples came tumbling down from the tree.

"Ow! Ouch!"

"Oh, dear! Are you all right, Julian?" Dr Gilbertson asked. "Who would've thought so much could happen on a fruit hunt."

When Pat arrived the children were just heading back to school.

"We've been on a fruit hunt," said Julian.

"Well, it certainly looks like you've found some. Oh, before I forget… I've got a parcel for you, Doctor."

"Oh, thanks, Pat. Oh…! My goodness, Pat. Where are your shoes today?"

Pat glanced down at his feet and wriggled the pink bunny slippers. "Oh, it's a long story," he said.

Pat and Jess arrive at the station café.

"Thanks for the letter, Pat," said Nisha. "Do you want a cup of tea?"

"Oh, no thanks, Nisha. I'm a bit late as it is."

Sara suddenly notices Pat's feet and laughs. "Erm… Pat…Do you know you're wearing pink fluffy slippers?"

"My feet got wet at the mill and these were all Ted had."

"Well, you can't wear those all day, Pat. I'll pop home and get you some dry shoes and socks."

"Thanks," said Pat. "That would be great. Can we meet at the school?"

Back at school the children gather all the different fruit they've collected and lay it out on a table in the playground.

Charlie, Julian, Meera and Lucy gather round the tomato plants.

"Lots of people think tomatoes are vegetables," said Charlie. "But they're not. They're a fruit actually."

"They've got loads of pips! Ugh!" said Julian. "How am I ever going to eat five pieces of fruit every day when I don't like any of these?"

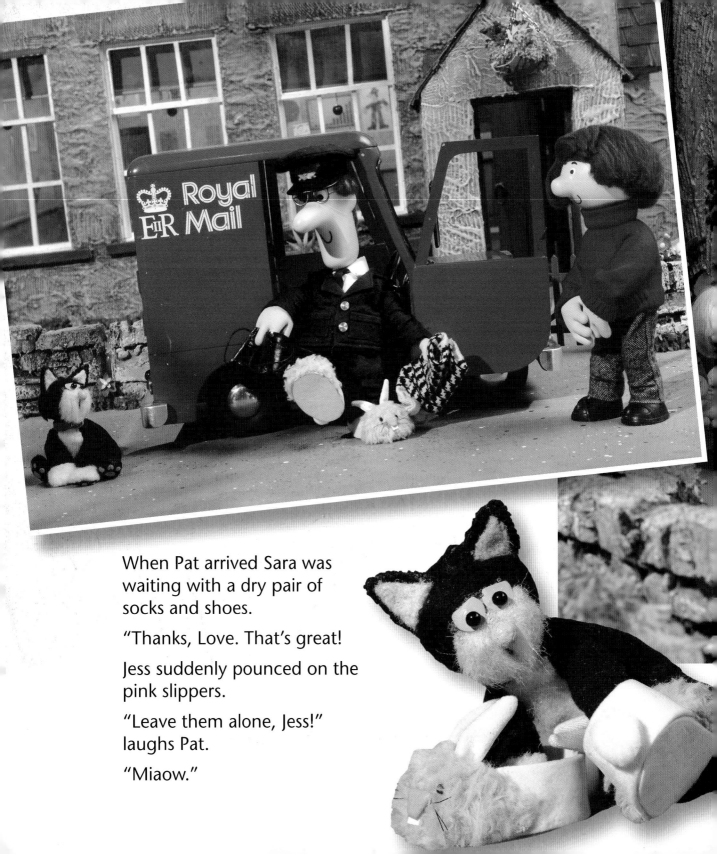

When Pat arrived Sara was waiting with a dry pair of socks and shoes.

"Thanks, Love. That's great!

Jess suddenly pounced on the pink slippers.

"Leave them alone, Jess!" laughs Pat.

"Miaow."

"Look at all this fruit we've collected, Pat," said Mr Pringle.
"That's wonderful."

Charlie was busy watering the tomatoes with Julian, Lucy and Meera.

"Watch out, Charlie!" cries Pat.

"Oops!" Charlie had accidentally poured water all over Pat's feet. "Ooh! Sorry, Pat."

"Oh, no!" cried Pat. "Not wet feet again!"

Just then Ted arrives with his sock-drying machine. "I've been looking everywhere for you, Pat," he said. "Oh… your feet are wet."

"I know… again!" Pat said.

"I've mended my new sock drying machine… so take those wet socks off, Pat, and I'll have 'em dry before you know it."

Everyone gathered round to watch. Jess jumped up onto the table knocking some of the fruit off into the sock machine.

"Oh, no, Jess!" cried Ted. "This machine's for socks, not fruit."

"Miaow!"

"Oh, dear, Ted! It's making a terrible mess!" said Mr Pringle.

"Hang on!" said Julian. He grabbed a cup and held it under the sock machine to catch the juice.

"Mmm. That's delicious. Let's make some more."

The children put all the different fruit in the sock-drying machine and caught all the juice in cups.

"Mmm," said Julian. "That tastes even better!"

"Well, I never!" Ted chuckles.

"It looks like you've found the perfect use for your sock-dryer after all, Ted." Pat laughs.

"Now the children can have their five pieces of fruit in one glass," Mr Pringle said.

"I'm sorry about your socks, Pat," said Ted.

Pat was wearing the pink slippers again. "Oh, it's ok, Ted."

"Cool slippers, Dad," said Julian.

"Thanks. Do you know, I think I'm getting rather used to them," laughs Pat, wriggling his toes.

SIMON AND SCHUSTER
First published in 2007 in Great Britain by Simon & Schuster UK Ltd
Africa House, 64-78 Kingsway
London WC2B 6AH
A CBS Company
A CIP catalogue record for this book is available from the British Library upon request

ISBN-13: 978-1-84738-002-9
Printed in China

1 3 5 7 9 10 8 6 4 2